The Last Campout

Prologue

Every July, as far back as Jadin could remember, her family went camping for a week at Comox Lake. It was the highlight of her summer vacation. She had precious memories of swimming in the crystal clear glacial fed waters there, being surrounded by forests and mountain views, staying up late around the campfire, and hiking the nearby trails. The last few weeks of the school year she had been filled with anticipation. She always left the Comox Lake campouts feeling refreshed, renewed, and happy. But this past year was different. She met an unusual boy named Andrew who changed her view of herself and the world she lived in.

Chapter 1

Andrew walked with the help of an aluminum cane. He wore a blue knitted toque to hide his baldness. Jadin spotted him the first morning at the campground, while his family laid out their towels on the beach. Andrew was thin. He moved as if he was in pain, slowly shuffling down to the sand at the water's edge. He plunged into the cool water and let out a joyful shout, tossing his cane to his father, who stood on the bank, cheering him on.

The chilly glacial fed lake soothed Andrew's pains. He smiled on the beach. When he entered the water, his smile turned into a laugh with shouts of joy. He swam until the skin on his fingers became wrinkled with a bluish tinge. After taking a break to lie out in the sun to warm up he did it again. When Jadin and her mother left to have lunch back at their campsite Andrew was still out dog paddling around the swimming raft anchored fifteen meters offshore.

Late in the afternoon Jadin met Andrew on one of the hiking trails. He was with his father, Ian, a tall man with a dark brown beard.

"Hi!" Jadin waved to Andrew as they crossed paths.

"Hi," Andrew said, stopping to lift his cane in greeting.

They continued their separate ways following a narrow winding trail through the old growth fir tree forest. Jadin was with her mother, headed back toward the campground. Andrew and his father were on the way to a waterfall located in the middle of a steep rock face that stretched for over a kilometer. In the early Spring the waterfall was a torrent. By summertime it was reduced to a trickle. The wooden bridge crossing the stream bed beneath it was made from rows of rough cedar planks, wide enough for one person to cross at a time.

When they returned to their campsite Jadin asked her mother about the boy who walked with the cane. Why was he bald?

"You should ask him," was Jadin's mother's reply.

The next opportunity to talk with Andrew came after supper while they were waiting in line at the campground snack shack. With a selection of hamburgers, hot dogs, poutine fries, and ice cream, it was a busy place on summer evenings.

After they received their orders, Jadin broke the silence, asking Andrew, "How long are you here for?"

Andrew took the first lick of his cookie dough ice cream cone. "We'll be here all week," he said, "We're leaving Sunday."

Jadin had medium poutine fries. She ate them out of a thin cardboard box with a plastic fork. "Us too," she spoke between mouthfuls. "We do this every summer. As long as I can remember we've been coming here."

They took seats across from each other at one of the picnic tables by the snack shack. After the usual introductions and talk of the great weather Jadin asked the question that was lingering in her heart. "Why do you walk with a cane?"

"I'm sick," Andrew replied, "I have weak legs."

"And your hair?"

"That's part of it too."

"The sickness made your hair fall out?"

Andrew spun the cone in his hand to lick the melting ice cream. "Yes," he swallowed.

"I hope you get better."

Andrew nodded. "Me too," he continued, "The cool lake water here eases the pain."

Jadin ate three more gravy and melted cheese curd covered fries. "Have you hiked out to Jacob's Ladder yet?"

"Jacob's ladder?"

"Yes, it's a lakeside cliff with all these spots you can jump off."

"How high?"

"The highest point is thirty meters. But I've never seen anyone jump off from there."

"How do you get there?"

"The trail you were on today with your father, keep following it all the way back out to the lake. Jacob's Ladder rises out of the lake there. There's a spot fifteen meters up where teenagers jump off. I'm thirteen this year so I'm going to jump off from there."

"Fifteen meters. That's high. Have you jumped before?"

"Yes, from five meters."

"I want to see this," Andrew said, setting the remains of his ice cream cone on a napkin. "Can we go there tomorrow? Will you show me?"

Jadin thought for a second. "Well, if your dad will let you."

"He will. We can meet-up here after lunch tomorrow, around one."

"Okay!" Jadin said and ate her last fries. "One-o-clock."

Andrew waited for an opportune time to ask for permission to go on the hike to Jacob's Ladder with Jadin. Seated on lawn chairs with his parents around their campfire that night, the stars overhead and the sweet scent of the burning cedar wood created the perfect atmosphere. The marshmallow fastened on the end of the thin wooden branch Andrew held over the coals took on the brown crust that could only be achieved by an experienced marshmallow toaster. Andrew let it cool off for a few seconds before he brought it to his mouth and ate it.

When he was finished, Andrew said, "Dad, I met a girl."

His father leaned forward in his lawn chair. "You met a girl?"

"Yes, she wants to go on a hike with me tomorrow."

Andrew's mother, Joanne, joined the conversation. "What's her name?"

"Her name's Jadin. She wants to meet me after lunch to hike to Jacob's Ladder."

Ian asked, "How far is that?"

"About two kilometers, there and back. It's at the end of the trail we were on yesterday, Dad."

Ian looked at his wife, Joanne. She smiled and nodded. "You can go but be careful. Take it slow."

"I will," Andrew promised.

That night it was after eleven by the time that Andrew got to sleep. Snuggled inside his sleeping bag, the only occupant of a two-man tent, he thought of Jadin and the adventure they had planned. He wondered if he had the courage to jump off Jacob's Ladder from the fifteen-meter height. Teenagers do it all the time, and he was almost one. In a couple of months, he would be thirteen. He thought, *"There's always next year."* But he doubted there would be a next year.

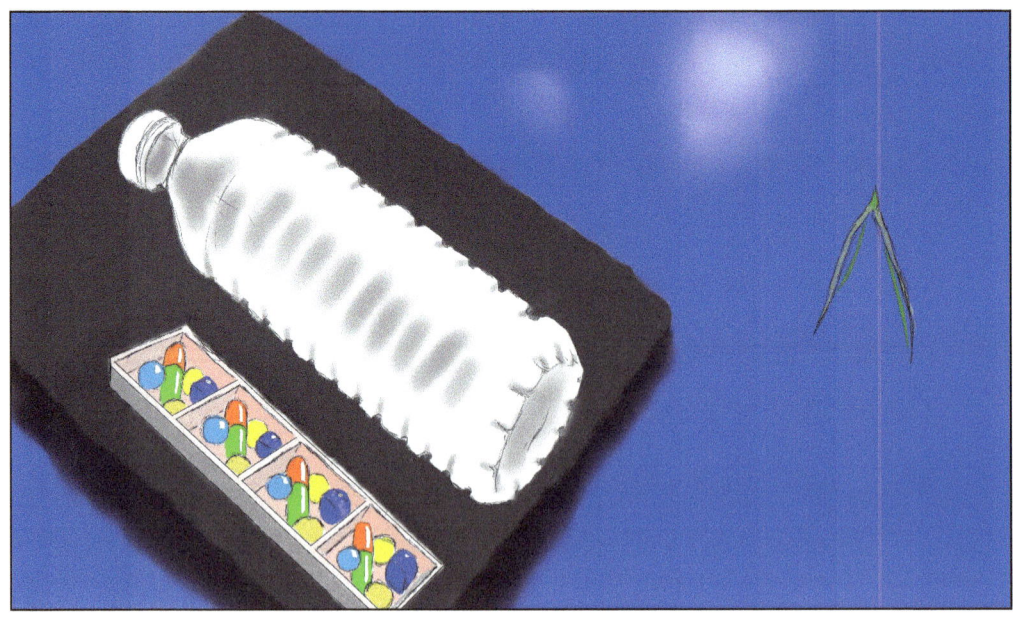

Chapter 2

Woken in the morning by the cry of an eagle, Andrew quickly crawled out of his tent to see if he could spot it. The bird was perched on the dead branches of a tall fir tree in the forest up the mountainside near the campground. He saw the eagle's white head as it caught the first rays of the early morning sun.

Andrew boiled a pot of water on the Coleman stove set up at the end of their picnic table. He liked to have hot oatmeal cereal, to get something warm into his belly to start the day. He had his morning medications to take, and he needed to do that with food. A blister pack containing ten pills of various colors and sizes was stored in a cooler inside their van. While the water boiled Andrew went to get it.

"Andrew!" Joanne called out from inside her tent, "Wait for a while after you eat before you go swimming."

"I will Mom," he assured her. She knew his plans. With the clear skies overhead, it would be the perfect morning to spend at the beach.

Jadin had made plans to go there too. She got up early to help her parents make breakfast. The scent of fried bacon and eggs lured the whole family out of their tents to gather around their campsite picnic table. Her mother, Shirley, father,

Ted, and younger sister, Janet, looked with anticipation toward Jadin as she used a metal spatula to serve the bacon and eggs. Everyone helped themselves to the toast, instant coffee, and orange juice Jadin had set out as part of the spread.

Once everyone began eating, Jadin announced, "I'm hiking to Jacob's ladder this afternoon with my new friend, Andrew."

"Oh, a boy," her father said. "Where did you meet him?"

"We met at the Snack Shack last night."

Shirley, Jadin's mom, listening in on the conversation, added, "That's the happy boy we saw on the beach yesterday, who walks with a cane. Did you find out why?"

"He says he's sick. His legs are weak."

Shirley looked concerned. "Is it safe for him to be going on the trails?"

"He said he wants to go. But I asked him to make sure it would be okay with his parents. But don't worry. We'll take it slow."

That morning Andrew joined a group of boys in a treasure hunt challenge on the beach. They had to look for hidden clues. Some were stored underwater in plastic bags near the swimming raft. Others were hidden, tied to the log booms that protected the cove swimming area from motorboats. Whoever found the last clue first, and the treasure, was declared the winner.

From her campsite Jadin heard the distant shouts and laughter of the boys on the beach. She recognized Andrew's voice and smiled knowing that he was having fun.

Andrew fell behind the other boys because he couldn't hold his breath long underwater. He had a mask and snorkel but because his lungs were weak, they were practically useless for diving to any depth. He cheered the others on.

At one-o-clock sharp, Andrew found Jadin waiting for him at a picnic table in the shade of the beach pavilion. She wore a light blue Tilley hat that matched Andrew's knitted toque. A grey knapsack was slung over her shoulder.

"I brought some snacks," Jadin said, rising to her feet, greeting Andrew.

"Excellent!" Andrew replied, lifting his aluminum cane into the air. "I put on my spiked tip. Gives me extra traction." He showed it to Jadin. "It screws on," Andrew said, twisting a small round black rubber latch on the end of his cane. "See."

They walked through the parking lot to the trail head that led into the forest. Old growth fir trees hid most of the massive rock-face they would hike along. The steep cliff with huge moss-covered boulders beneath it appeared after a hundred meters. Jadin slowed her walking pace so Andrew could catch up. Andrew commented, that one of the rock formations had the face of an old man. Jadin recognized this for the first time, saying, "Oh yes, that's his big nose and eyebrows."

They both laughed and continued. "Look for newts. I've found some before here," Jadin explained. "They love to crawl on these mossy logs."

"What's a newt?"

"It's a type of salamander. Their skin is light green with brown spots."

"Oh, yes," Andrew remembered. "I've seen one before down by the lake, in the mud at the creek."

A few minutes later, as they approached a narrow wooden bridge over a dried-up stream bed, Jadin caught a newt. It was as long as her hand. She held it out for Andrew to see. The newt's head moved back and forth with quick jerky motions.

"Nice one," Andrew complemented Jadin.

"Here," Jadin said, passing the newt to Andrew.

He held out his hand as she set it on his palm. "The feet are so soft," Andrew laughed, "I've never actually held one before." He passed it back to Jadin.

She patted it on the head and then gently set the newt down on a lush green leaf.

They stopped to rest on a log further along the trail. Jadin could tell that Andrew was struggling. "Let's sit," she said. "What's causing all the pain?"

"The bones in my legs," Andrew replied, as he sat down. "The blood doesn't flow through them properly. The bone marrow is damaged."

"How is it damaged?"

There was an uncomfortable silence.

Andrew sighed, "I have cancer."

"That's serious," she replied, wanting to ask more questions but she could see that Andrew was hesitant to continue.

"I know," Andrew said. "Let's get going. I want to see you jump off Jacob's Ladder." He brushed dried pine needles off his shorts, standing up.

They continued to follow the narrow trail through the forest at the base of the cliff. At one point they had to use a rope to climb up a steep rock face. A series of narrow wooden bridges and steps finally led them to Jacob's Ladder, a fifty-meter cliff at the lake's edge.

Andrew used the spike in his walking stick for support as he climbed with Jadin to the five-meter ledge. They sat together with their legs dangling down. Jadin took a clear plastic bag out of her knapsack. A sandwich and some pickles were inside. "My mom made it for us."

"We shouldn't eat before we swim," Andrew cautioned.

"We're in no hurry," Jadin laughed. "The lake's not going anywhere."

"Okay," Andrew gave in, taking half of the summer sausage sandwich.

The sun in the cloudless midday sky caused the calm lake waters below them to mirror the surrounding mountains. They ate, while taking in the view. Jadin pointed to two eagles perched in the top branches of an old fir tree across the lake. Flying much higher up the mountainside on the thermals without flapping their wings they had landed there to rest.

"Where do you go to school?" Andrew asked Jadin.

"On the mainland, North Vancouver. I can walk there from our house. What about you?"

"I'm home schooled. We live in the Comox Valley, not far from here."

"You're educated at home? Must be nice."

"I've only been doing it for two years. Since I became ill. I missed too many classes because I was in hospital. I fell behind."

"Sad."

"Not really. My mom is my teacher. She lets me have an extra-long lunch break. Sometimes we watch weekday movie matinees with retirees."

Jadin ate the last bite of her sandwich. "Do you want to see where the teens jump off?"

"Sure," Andrew answered, crumpling the saran wrap he had in his hand into a ball. Not wanting to litter, he put it into his pocket after standing up.

"Be careful Andrew. The next section is steep."

"I will."

They slowly climbed higher on Jacob's Ladder to fifteen meters. The ledge at that height was narrow and moss covered. Andrew had to lean out to see where the cliff jumpers would splash into the crystal-clear lake water. It seemed so far down.

"Do you think I can do it?" Jadin asked Andrew.

"That's pretty high up."

"Other teenagers do, and I'm a teenager now."

Andrew tossed a pebble off the ledge and watched it fall. He heard it plunk into the water. "That's a long way. How about we both jump from the five-meter height today."

"You'll do it with me?"

"Yes."

"You're going to love it."

"I've never jumped off a cliff before, just a diving board at a pool."

"Remember those eagles we saw?"

"Yeah."

"You're going to feel the sensation of flight, like them."

"Cool," Andrew said as he started the descent of the steep trail. The spike in his cane came in handy at the first step down, where he needed extra support.

Once they reached the five-meter height they removed their running shoes and socks. Jadin planned to be the first to jump.

"On the count of three," Jadin said, pumping her arms. "One. Two. Three!" she shouted, leaping off the cliff. She flew out over some small evergreens that clung to the steep rockface, and continued down, splashing into the water. She hollered after coming to the surface, pumping her fist into the air.

Andrew's heartrate jumped as he shuffled closer to the edge. He peered down, hesitant. Jadin looked excited.

"Come on!" Jadin called out, dog paddling. "You can do it!"

Suddenly, courage welled up in Andrew and he leapt out into the air. He felt the sensation of flight remembering what Jadin had said. It was true. This feeling of exhilaration came just before his fall was broken by the cool crystal-clear lake water. He went down underwater a couple of meters, holding his breath. Jadin took his hand as he surfaced. She swam with him back to the shore.

"That was amazing," Andrew huffed, out of breath.

They sat on a boulder at the foot of Jacob's Ladder to dry out in the afternoon sun.

"I'm going to jump from fifteen meters," Andrew proclaimed.

"You can," Jadin agreed. "Next year you'll be thirteen. You'll be a teenager. You can do it then."

"I want to do it this summer before I leave. I might not be here next year."

"Why? Are you moving?"

"No." Andrew hesitated. It was hard for him to say. "The type of cancer I have can't be cured. The doctors say I'm dying. I don't have long to live."

"No!" Jadin stood up. "There's got to be something they can do…"

"I'm not afraid to die. I know where I'm going."

"Well," Jadin made a fist.

"Don't be angry. We're all dying. Some of us are just dying faster than others."

"How can you be alright with this?" Jadin almost shouted.

"I know that heaven is real. I believe what the Bible says. It's true…"

"You do seem happy."

"I am," Andrew smiled. "I know there's a purpose for my life that's beyond this world."

Jadin helped Andrew to stand. She walked with him, supporting one of his arms as they climbed up the cliff to retrieve their socks and running shoes. "So, you want to jump from fifteen meters, tomorrow?" she asked.

Andrew nodded, saying, "I do."

Their wet clothing had dried off by the time that they had reached the campground. Andrew felt elated, knowing that he had completed the jump from five meters.

After supper at their campsite, as Andrew sat at the picnic table with his father, he shared the news.

"You jumped off Jacob's Ladder!" His father, Ian, was in awe. "Amazing! I've kayaked by there. That's a high cliff."

"We jumped from five meters."

"Jadin jumped off too?"

"Yes, she did."

"How was it?"

"I felt like an eagle in flight."

"How were your legs?"

"Like usual. I had to rest a couple of times while hiking on the trail out and back. Jadin helped me on the steep parts," Andrew smiled, remembering this time when Jadin took his hand on the way back. They held hands for a few minutes, walking on a steep decline. "I like her."

"You like her?"

"I do. She's fun to be around. She knows the truth Dad, and she still wants to be around me."

"You told her about the cancer?"

"Yes, she kept asking. She wants to hike out there with me again tomorrow."

"Can you handle that?"

"Yes, if I get a good night's sleep and take my medications, I can."

"Are you sure? I don't want you to get hurt."

"I won't," Andrew assured his dad.

Before they lit the campfire that night Jadin helped her mother, Shirley, to wash up the stainless-steel camping dishes. They used two separate Tupperware storage bins; one for hot soapy water, and one for the colder rinse water. Once they were clean, they were laid out on a dish towel to air dry.

"We're going to jump off Jacob's Ladder again, tomorrow," Jadin told her mom. "I'm jumping from where I've never jumped before."

"You and your new friend?"

"Yes, Andrew."

"Doesn't he have a disability? Should he be doing something like that?"

"He likes it. He wants to," Jadin reflected, scrubbing the frying pan. She set it in the rinse water. "He told me that he's dying soon, that he might not live to see next summer, when he'll be a teenager."

Shirley reached out to Jadin and hugged her. They had tears in their eyes. "That's so sweet of you to help him."

Jadin paused to think, and said, "He has helped me more than I have helped him."

"How's that?"

"Andrew has this faith that's so genuine. He's not afraid of dying."

"Why?"

"He says heaven is real, that the Bible is true, and that there's a purpose for his life beyond this world."

"And you believe him?" Shirley hung the wash rag in her hand over a clothesline tied between two nearby trees. "Have you ever read the Bible?"

"I've read some of it online before…"

"And what did you think?"

"I thought it was just some ancient stories. Have you ever read it?"

"Years ago. It didn't make much sense to me. But if it gives Andrew hope, it can't be bad," Shirley said, hugging her daughter around the shoulder. "You're becoming quite the young lady."

"Thanks Mom," Jadin replied. She went to sit by the campfire with the rest of the family.

Chapter 3

An early morning mist settled upon Comox Lake. When Andrew awoke, he found the sides of his tent were drenched. The running shoes that he left outside were too. The shoes were chilly to put on. He needed them to protect his bare feet from the gravel as he walked with his cane to the van where the cooking supplies were stored. He was excited to start the day with a good breakfast, so he got a pot of water boiling on the Coleman stove and prepared to make a bowl of hot oatmeal.

The rising sun burned off the mist. Eventually Andrew's parents, Ian, and Joanne, awoke, and joined him at the picnic table. The blister pack containing ten pills that Andrew had to take was set out before him.

Ian sipped a hot cup of coffee. "So, this is the big day," he spoke to Andrew. "You're going to jump off from fifteen meters."

Andrew smiled, saying, "That's the plan. I'm meeting Jadin at ten and we'll hike out there."

"Do you mind if we come to watch? We'll cheer you on."

Joanne nodded, saying, "I'll take photos."

Andrew took two pills with water. He gulped, and asked, "You don't have other plans?"

"We were going to go into town for some fresh baked donuts. But we can do that after, to celebrate."

Andrew figured Jadin would like extra company. "Okay!" he agreed.

Andrew's parents followed from a distance, watching their son, as he hiked along the forest trail with Jadin. They were pleased to see him so happy, even though they knew he was struggling. The cane that Andrew used helped to keep him stable.

Jadin caught another newt by the dried-up stream. She waited for Andrew's parents so she could show them. "We found another newt!" Andrew hollered. Joanne pulled out her smart phone and took a photo of Ian holding it. It looked like the newt had smiled for the camera.

As they neared Jacob's Ladder Ian noticed a bird nest in the lowest branches of a young cedar tree. It was small and intricately constructed with twigs and mud. He pointed it out to Jadin. "See the bird nest? How did the bird know how to build it?"

Jadin thought for a second. "Their mother taught them?" she replied.

"No," Ian went on to explain, "The bird intuitively knows how to build the bird nest. The hummingbird that constructed this was born with the knowledge."

"Wow! That's amazing," Jadin exclaimed.

"Yes, it reminds me of how the Holy Spirit intuitively knows how to build God's kingdom in our lives."

"The Holy Spirit?" Jadin asked, "What is that?"

"He descended on Jesus Christ in the form of a dove when he was baptized by John the Baptist a little over two-thousand years ago in Israel. The Holy Spirit came upon Jesus' disciples after he ascended to heaven," Ian spoke to them all as they stood on the trail by the tree.

"Oh," Jadin reflected, "I didn't know that."

Joanne added, "And the Holy Spirit works with believers still today. He's also called the helper because He helps us to walk in the truth."

This was all too new to Jadin. She didn't know what to say, but she determined that she would give this matter serious thought later.

Andrew heard the echoing shouts of two teenagers paddling a kayak in the lake below them. He couldn't see them through the thick undergrowth. As he and Jadin ascended Jacob's Ladder to the fifteen-meter cliff edge the kayakers came into sight. Because of the echoes they had sounded closer than they were. From the ledge Andrew saw an orange twin kayak far off in the middle of the lake. With each stroke they took the bright morning sun flashed across their wet paddles.

Ian and his wife Joanne waited at the base of the cliff. Joanne had her smartphone out and was lining up the best angle to take photos of the jump.

Andrew removed his socks and shoes, saying, "I'm going to jump first." He set his cane down on the ledge.

"Okay," Jadin spoke with a tone of concern, "I'll take your things down."

"Wait here 'til I go, please."

"Okay."

"Count down with me," Andrew continued.

"Three, two, one!" they both shouted.

Andrew leapt. As if in slow motion he fell, raising his arms to keep balanced like a soaring eagle. The sensation of flight lasted longer this time. The excitement of the jump almost caught him off-guard. He remembered at the last second to tuck his arms back against his hips before splashing down into the water. The sudden envelope of coolness was exhilarating. After swimming up and breaking through the surface Andrew pumped a fist into the air. "Yahooo!" he shouted.

Joanne was able to get three good photos of Andrew's jump.

As Andrew swam to the shore, Jadin brought down his cane, socks and running shoes. When they met on the narrow lakeshore beneath the cliff they shared a celebratory hug.

"It's your turn now," Andrew told Jadin. "You'll love it."

Jadin took a deep breath. "I'm going to do it."

Jadin scrambled quickly up Jacob's Ladder to the fifteen-meter ledge. Andrew watched from below as she prepared to jump. He put one hand up to shield his eyes from the bright midday sun.

"One, two, three …" Jadin shouted, and leapt. She too felt the sensation of flight, soaring through the air. It would be a milestone in her life. Her first jump as a teenager. As she splashed into the water this feeling of contentment rushed over her. Jadin had accomplished one of the most important goals of her summer vacation. Somehow it had exceeded what she had imagined because she was able to share it with Andrew. She believed that he was dying and was pleased to have played a part in bringing more joy to his life.

Andrew shouted when he saw Jadin surface. "Yeah!" He pumped his arm into the air. "Way to go!"

Later, Jadin and Andrew celebrated by sharing a box of freshly baked donuts with Ian and Joanne at the little bakery on main street in the nearby village of Cumberland. Andrew's parents treated them. They sat around a small storefront table.

"We're proud of you both," Ian spoke, taking the first bite of his glazed donut. "They're still warm."

"Yummy!" Andrew smiled taking his second bite.

After finishing her donut Jadin licked her fingertips, and said, "It's weird to think that after a couple of days we might not ever see each other again."

"You never know," Ian replied. "God could heal Andrew."

"How?" Jadin asked.

Joanne answered, "By giving us a miracle."

Ian added, "We're praying for one."

Jadin bit into a second donut, deep in thought. "I want to pray for a miracle too," Jadin said. "How can I?"

"By believing in what Jesus said," Ian explained. "Have you read the Bible? In the New Testament Jesus says that those who believe in him will be able to do the same things that He did with the help of the Holy Spirit."

"I've read some of that before …"

"Do you believe it?"

Jadin thought a second, and said, "I didn't then, but I do now."

"You can pray. Ask by faith."

"I want to pray. I want to help. I don't want Andrew to die."

"If you believe - you can pray."

"I've never prayed before. How do I do it?"

Ian replied, "Talk to God just like you're talking to us."

Jadin set her hand on Andrew's shoulder, saying, "God, I've never prayed before so if I don't do it right forgive me. I believe you can heal Andrew like you healed those other people in the Bible. So that's what I'm asking you to do. Please heal Andrew of this cancer…"

"Amen!" Ian and Joanne agreed.

To receive from heaven, Andrew held both of his hands up, one holding a half-eaten donut.

Joanne had tears running down her cheeks. "That was a beautiful prayer, Jadin."

Some people passing by on the sidewalk stopped to take in this rare expression of public prayer. An older man stopped to bow his head and nodded.

When it was done Ian said, "Thanks!" He hugged Jadin around the shoulder.

Cloudy weather didn't stop Jadin from taking their kayak out on the lake the last morning they spent at the campground. Birds called to each other in the early morning light as she slid the orange twin kayak off the old cedar plank dock at the camp's tuck shop and wharf. The first one out on the water that day, she had a feeling of solitude. But she knew she was not alone. Jesus was with her. She felt the joy of the Holy Spirit's presence. A new contentment came over her.

Andrew waved when he saw Jadin kayak by as he walked on the beach with his dad. They had to break camp by eleven to make room for new vacationers. This was their last visit to the lake's bank this summer.

"Do you think it's going to rain?" Andrew asked his dad.

Ian peered up to the clouds. "They should pass by," he said. "But just in case we should take down the tents, and pack things away in the van."

"I'll make breakfast," Andrew offered, as he turned to head back to their campsite. He quickened his walking pace, keeping balanced with the help of his cane.

Andrew knew well the routine of breaking camp. He rolled up his sleeping bag, stuffed his clothes into his backpack, along with any toiletries or reading materials. The last step involved the packing of the tent. This had to be folded and rolled while taking care to brush away any pine needles or dirt clinging to the fabric. Ian helped Andrew to tightly roll the tent and stuff it into its storage sack. The family worked as a team and soon the van was fully packed.

The campground manager came by to check them out of their site. He felt the ashes inside the fire ring with his fingertips to make sure they were doused. There was no trash left on the ground. They were good to go.

Near eleven they drove away, heading to the exit by the camp tuck shop. Jadin and her family were there too, in their van. Andrew opened his window to talk with

Jadin as she waved to him and was saying something, but he couldn't hear.

"What can I do?" Jadin called out.

Andrew shouted back, "Keep praying for me."

"I will," Jadin promised.

They vowed to keep in contact through e-mail.

With kayaks and gear bags strapped to their roof racks the vans left the Comox Lake campground driving up the narrow lakeside road that would lead them through the village of Cumberland and back to the highway.

Epilogue

This ended up being the last campout at Comox Lake for Jadin and her family as they moved overseas after becoming Christian missionaries in southwest Asia.

Andrew returned to Comox Lake and continued to jump from Jacob's Ladder every summer until he left home for college. God heard Jadin's prayer and healed Andrew of his cancer. He grew back a full head of thick brown hair and he no longer walked with a cane.

Andrew and Jadin still stay in contact through e-mail. Who knows what the future holds?

Milton Keynes UK
Ingram Content Group UK Ltd.
UKHW050155150824
446876UK00019B/52